Incessantly Bigfooting Through Time

More Light-Hearted Stories from a Lifelong Bigfoot Enthusiast

Kevin Llewellyn

Rusty Truck Publishing—Spokane, WA
ISBN: 979-8-9856917-1-9
Library of Congress Control Number: 2023902240
Title: *Incessantly Bigfooting Through Time: More Light-Hearted Stories from a Lifelong Bigfoot Enthusiast*
Author: Kevin Llewellyn
Digital distribution | 2023
Paperback | 2023

This is a work of fiction. The characters, names, incidents, places, and dialogue are products of the author's imagination, and are not to be construed as real.

Dedication

This book is dedicated to my dad who spent many hours with me in the forest and on the water. He taught me to enjoy the magnificence of nature and respect it. This is also dedicated to my wife, Carol. I cherish her support and interest in my pursuits (and the great homemade cookies and snacks she has for me when I return home from a long camping trip!)

Table of Contents

Introduction

I was fortunate at ten years of age to see Roger Patterson present in person the Patterson-Gimlin film at the Spokane Coliseum in Spokane, Washington. I got his autograph that night. Later, I became a member of his Northwest Research Association and received bulletins/newsletters that he wrote.

Through the decades, I have had many encounters and experiences that I can only attribute to Bigfoot activity. I do question everything I hear and see. Every investigator has their own approach. My approach is to have respect for the forest and Bigfoot. I try many things to both make Bigfoot curious about me and feel comfortable to approach. Over the years, I have a list of things I do and have had good luck. Whatever works for you, keep doing it.

This book continues with more light-hearted stories following my first book, **Incessantly Bigfooting.** Many are based on my Bigfoot experiences and other stories are based on Bigfoot behavior added for your enjoyment.

Part One
More Light-Hearted Stories

The Cabin

I was young and this was my first extended hunting trip for forest grouse. My cousin that was also very young, his father and I arrived in a tent trailer in the mountains the day before the season opener.

Far across the meadow was an old cabin. How many decades had this structure been there? The wood was a combination of weathered gray and black from decay. Whoever built it, made it to withstand time and the roof was intact. The closed door still hung strong to its frame. That afternoon, I looked at the cabin with many questions. What happened to the homesteaders? How long were they here? What struggles did they endure? What wildlife did they encounter? The shadows grew long in the late afternoon and crept over the cabin.

We were busy around camp preparing to stay for several days of hunting. At sunset, I looked across the meadow and saw the cabin door wide open. Confusion and curiosity set in. There was no wind.

"Let's go over and look in the cabin," my cousin said.

"Seriously?" I questioned. "We may come face-to-face with a bear! Something grabbed that door to open it!"

"I'll stay here and watch you two," his father said. 'If you want to go check it out but I don't think there is anything to see. It's an old cabin falling apart."

"I'm going, are you?"

"I'll go if you go!"

After much debate, courage began to grow. Maybe, neither one of us wanted to appear afraid nor being chicken. We each grabbed a flashlight and started toward the cabin. It was getting darker by the minute. As we came close to the open door, I thought maybe being chicken about this was actually the logical approach.

We paused at the entrance, then stepped into the dark cabin. Our flashlights lit up the one room cabin. The wooden floor had many holes and revealed years of droppings from wood rats. The musty odor of dampness, uncleanliness and age made me want to back out. In the back of the cabin was a large pile of dried grass. Probably from years of wood rats collecting it. But, could something else have brought it into the cabin?

We had overcome our fears and figuring out how the door opened was secondary. We went back to camp in the dark feeling invincible and looking forward to hunting grouse in the morning.

I went outside the tent trailer one last time before trying to get some sleep. The stars were incredible filling the clear sky and the full moon was rising above the mountain to the east. I will never forget the howl that pierced the autumn night. Coyote? No, it was very different than a coyote howl. It was haunting. It called to me. I was not afraid. The next time I heard such a howl would be many years later as a newlywed. But, the next day was my first day paying more attention to anything in the woods that seemed out-of-place from the common forest animals or natural occurrences. While looking for grouse, I vowed to begin seeing everything in the forest, as much as possible. To observe more than just trees, streams and wildlife trails. My future was full of hunting and camping trips with my dad and that meant countless days to be observant in the woods.

To this day, I vividly remember that old cabin in the shadows with the foreboding black square of the open door, the full moon over the mountain and that call. The call seemed to connect with something ancient in me, pulling me back to a time when everything lived in the forest. There is something out there. This was one of the first steps on my quest to find out what is wild, free, mysterious and undiscovered in the forests.

The Quest Continues

The cold water of the mountain stream felt good on that hot July morning. It was not deep but I could feel the power of the current on the side of my calves. I had left my shoes on for traction but I still had visions of twisting or breaking an ankle. Wading across the stream was the only way to enter a prime Bigfoot habitat area. These are the places I like to explore: places where few people go.

Safely across the stream, we picked up a trail that many, many years ago was an old logging road or access for fighting wildfire. It was now overgrown to the point of being a wildlife trail through the trees and brush. It did not take long and someone thought they heard voices to our right. This paralleling encounter continued as we hiked up the trail traveling deeper into the Washington Cascade Mountains.

In addition to possible voices, we heard branch breaks, twig snaps and thumps. These were always 45 degrees to our right behind us or in front as we moved along. We continued to hike and talk about what we were hearing. We did not do any Bigfoot vocalizations but allowed the encounter to continue. We discussed if it was Bigfoot, the thumping sounds may be from chest pounding. Maybe a Bigfoot picked up a large rock and dropped it on the ground or an exposed tree root at different times, rather than throwing it. Maybe a Bigfoot stomped its foot, although I think there was enough distance between us that we would not hear that.

In my first book, **Incessantly Bigfooting**, I mentioned that it is best to have two or more Bigfoot related activities, different vocalizations, or findings occur. This tips the scale in favor of Bigfoot. I also like to do recreations. How do you recreate a paralleling encounter? Go back to the area under the same weather conditions at the same time of day. We went back the next morning, no change to the weather. We did not hear any of the sounds that we experienced the previous morning.

I love the mystery of Bigfoot. I will continue my quest to learn more about their behavior and try to increase my chances of encounters and sightings.

Next, are more light-hearted stories. Also, stories that follow Bigfoot activity on a fictitious ranch over one hundred years.

Cast Material

There are great types of cast material to make casts of possible Bigfoot tracks. The casts harden fairly quickly and are strong. The worst thing that could happen to a great cast of a possible Bigfoot footprint would be if it breaks apart.

During mixing, the cast material may need to vary from thicker to watery. It depends on the type of soil the track was left in and if the track is on a steep hillside. In my first book, **Incessantly Bigfooting,** I described making the cast associated with my sighting. I began to panic as I watched some cast material run downhill from the track. But I had the correct consistency and the cast turned out well.

Because I never know what conditions a track will be found in, I like to practice casting other animal tracks. I have some cougar casts that show the claws. I once cast wild turkey tracks in mud. A poult was following a hen. When looking at the cast of their feet, they remind me of miniature dinosaur tracks.

One thing I have learned over the years, it takes more material to make the cast than what I first thought. I don't want to guess at how many pounds I am using. Therefore, I have pre-weighed bags of one kilogram. As a result of practice, I have an idea of how many pounds it will take to cast a particular track.

I always carry casting material but, what if it might be confused with something else as in this fictitious story.

One morning my friend said, "Let's make pancakes and afterward drive to that trailhead and hike the trail." I have everything except eggs and flour."

"The eggs are in my cooler and the flour in the back of my truck," I answered while changing batteries in some equipment.

"Oh no, what is going on?" my friend shouted a few minutes later.

"What's happening?" I said with a worried tone. I was now removing the twenty trail cameras that were on my truck from the night before so we could drive to the trailhead.

"The pancake batter just began solidifying!"

I looked at the bowl. In it was a rock hard mass.

"I think that's casting material and not flour!" I exclaimed.

My friend had also dumped in some chocolate chips and some were sitting solid in the surface of the hardened material.

"If we play connect the chips, does that look like the outline of a Bigfoot?" I wondered.

"I think it looks like a bear – with fangs!"

"Do you need a weight to hold down a tarp?" I asked, trying to be positive. "Are there any eggs left?"

Campfires Through Time

Bigfooting means camping. After camping for decades, I have seen a lot of different ways to build and start a campfire.

There are many types of campfire designs. Some examples are; log cabin, teepee, platform, star, parallel, lean-to, keyhole. Also, there is the very popular just throw on some wood. This is usually the case when no chainsaw or axe is available and the wood varies from the size of matchsticks to uprooted tree stumps that have been gathered throughout the forest. It is also the case when the conversation is so riveting, nobody cares about the shape of the fire, just as long as there are flames. The Swedish torch fire is not necessarily "built" as it is a vertically set trunk, cut down from the top and burns in the middle. Some members of my family, rather than making a Swedish torch, would rather stand a hollow log in the middle of the fire!

More varied than the type of campfire, is the way to light one. Over the years, I have seen people use many different techniques for starting.

From the "bird's nest" bundle of dry material, to the next step of cheating with wadded newspaper or paper wrapped logs. Then, if there is a little pyromania involved, fire starter gels and liquid are used. There are many more techniques. I have used many fire starting techniques, but never rubbed two sticks together. I do need to mention one underused, quirky technique in the following story. Have you started a fire with snack names that end in "itos" or "eetos?" They do burn – trust me! [CAUTION: do not use the entire bag!]

There had been drenching rain for many hours. It stopped just when we arrived at our campsite. After setting up our tents, my friend and I discussed the difficulty of starting a fire with everything so wet.

"Nothing is dry!" my fellow investigator said.

"Yes, everything is soaked and I did not bring any newspaper. I have a fire starting cube for emergency purposes," I said as I munched some chips. (They are my favorite chip and always have some with me on camping trips.)

"Well, let's use those," my friend stated.

"My chips? Well, maybe a few."

"Because everything is so wet, dump the whole bag out!"

"The whole bag of my favorite chips?"

"Do you want to eat chips or have a campfire?" he asked. "I brought chocolate chip cookies!"

I thought, "That's a great trade!"

One must be careful with the campfire. That includes drying your clothing with the heat. I have seen many tennis shoes and boots start smoldering and melting in their place on the fire ring. This discussion includes clothing that is on your body. Once, we were camping on an island in the middle of a lake. We had the fire in a safe location, but the fire may have been a little large! I think it lit up the lake from end to end. If there was any Bigfoot around, they may not have liked the bright light. One person decided to lay on the ground with his back to the fire. All of a sudden, his insulated coveralls began smoldering on his back. He could not get out of the coveralls fast enough.

Of course, where there is fire, there is smoke. Why does the smoke always blow on me only? Or, at least it seems that way. It is a pain in my eyes! My clothes (and me) always smell of smoke. I don't know if that covers my scent so I can get closer to Bigfoot or if Bigfoot smells my smoky presence in the woods more easily. I would continue to study this, except I always smell of smoke because the smoke finds me no matter where I sit around the campfire.

It is great to get away and go camping. But, a campfire is a must to unwind and enjoy the company of your fellow investigators.

Henry David Thoreau said, "The fire is the main comfort of the camp, whether in summer or winter, and is about as ample at one season as at another. It is as well for cheerfulness as for warmth and dryness."

Ghost Stories

When hoping to have a Bigfoot encounter, a person has to be persistent about getting into the woods. However, most of the time, there is not any Bigfoot activity when camping and scouting for them. When there is no Bigfoot activity to discuss, many varied stories are told around a campfire.

The campfire was extra pleasant to gather around because it was cold, damp and foggy that night in the mountains. The night before had been clear and moonless. We were camped in a spot that had a spooky feeling to us. But, that did not give rise to any Bigfoot activity.

As the three of us sat around the campfire, I decided to make up a ghost story with what I had supposedly seen on my way to camp the night before.

"You know, last night when I was down the road a bit driving here, I saw something spooky cross the road! The road crested ahead of me with the stars beyond. This black figure crossed the road, paused at the edge and was gone. It blocked out the stars!"

"A Bigfoot?" my one friend exclaimed.

"No, it was not walking. It was – like – floating. I was in disbelief!"

I had my friends' attention. They bought into my story as if it was true. My other friend excitedly began relaying his knowledge of the area history.

"Well, I read about an ornery man that was a miner and trapper. His cabin was somewhere around here. The story goes that he hated people. He supposedly ran explorers off the mountain with an axe. When I talked to other Bigfoot investigators about this area, I heard that his ghost has been seen around here. His ghost chases campers just like he chased explorers when he was alive. Maybe he didn't want people up here because he was protecting Bigfoot. Anyway, his spirit is still here and it is angry! Maybe he is still trying to protect Bigfoot, even as a ghost."

My friend that asked if I saw a Bigfoot exclaimed, "Something just touched my ear!"

"Oh come on," I said. "I made that up about the black figure last night. I really did see a black figure cross a county road once. My wife was with me and saw it, too. Very mysterious!" I added.

"This place gives me the creeps!" he said while rubbing his ear and looking behind him. "Look!" he shouted. A swirl of mist came from behind, drawing closer to him.

"That's fog swirling around," I stated. "But, if it makes you feel better, I'll put the axe in my truck for the night."

"I'm cold," they both said almost simultaneously.

"It is cold and damp tonight," I stated. "No more talk about ghosts."

"Something just touched my shoulder! It is true what other investigators told me. There's another mist figure!"

"Really, I made that up about seeing a black figure last night!" I repeated. "I'm putting the axe in my truck and then headed into my tent."

A loud, moaning howl rang out from close by and it stopped me in my tracks half way to my truck. I thought it would never stop. After placing the sheath on the axe, I put it in the cab of my truck.

One of my friends exclaimed, "That was not a coyote! How am I going to get any sleep? I need some whiskey!"

"I didn't bring any, did you guys?" I asked.

"No."

Anxiety filled the air. I tried to break the tension and said humorously, "No one talk in their sleep tonight!"

The next morning remained foggy as I heard my friends getting out of their tents. As I got out of my tent, I saw them near my truck looking at the ground. I walked over and a chill hit me. I stared in disbelief. There on the ground was my axe – without the sheath! All the truck doors were closed. I was awake all night and never heard the sound of a door open or close.

"I'm outta here!" I said after staring at the axe for I don't know how long. I turned around and my friends were already dropping their tents.

We packed in a flurry. No one said a word but I thought, "No way will I be a ghost hunter, I'll continue to investigate Bigfoot!"

As I started to get in my truck to leave, I remembered my audio recorder was still behind camp. Another long, mournful howl came from that direction. My recorder may still be there.

Microzoophobia And Walkie Talkies

When you camp with someone for several days in the mountains, you may learn certain things about them you would not know if say, they were your neighbor in the city. One category is phobias. I have seen people react with panic to certain creatures, even just the mention of one. For example, I mention I saw a field mouse on my thermal imager run through camp and someone panics. Microzoophobia is the fear of small animals. More specific phobias include; arachnophobia (fear of spiders), chiroptophobia (fear of bats), ophidiophobia (fear of snakes), spheksophobia (fear of wasps), musophobia (fear of mice and rats.) Hippopotomonstrosesquippedaliophobia is one of the longest words in the dictionary and is the name for fear of long words. Really, look it up!

Walkie Talkies are the bane of my Bigfooting equipment. I want to hike quietly through the forest and I disdain the squawking sounds that come from walkie talkies. However, they are an important safety item to have when your Bigfooting group divides up in different directions. If someone becomes injured, they can report such over the walkie talkie.

A circumstance may arise when both microzoophobia and walkie talkies are involved.

"What channel are we on?" someone asked as we were gathering our equipment to leave camp soon.

"The usual," I replied just before the panicked person came running up to the campfire ring.

"There is something in my tent!" they exclaimed. "What do I do? I heard it inside!"

We walked up to their tent. It was close to sunset and shadows were moving over the tent.

"There is a mouse in there and I'm freaked out. I hate mice! As you see, I did not get the tent door completely closed at the bottom," the tent owner fearfully announced.

A slight breeze made one tent wall wiggle and someone said, "That's bigger than a mouse. It may be a skunk."

"I'm going to faint! How do we get it out? There, did you hear that?"

"I did hear a squeak," I answered. But, after seeing the tent owner shaking, maybe I should not say anything more and open the tent. My mind was filled with visions of opening the tent door and being face-to-face with a skunk or a mean raccoon. As the sound repeated I said, "Wait - I have heard that before."

I opened the tent door, confident I knew what was going on. The owner gasped as I stepped inside.

"Here's what is making the sound," I said. "Your walkie talkie volume is so low and a couple of youngsters are on this channel. You can barely hear them but they are chatting back and forth nonstop. We are hearing this low squawking coming from the walkie talkie. I have had this happen several times. We need to change to a different channel."

The breathing of the tent owner with musophobia was returning to normal.

"Oh crap! Was that a bat?" someone shouted!!!

Men of the Mountains Revisited

The storm was raging outside. Rain was pelting the shack. It was coming in torrents with howling wind gusts adding to the storm's assault on the old shanty. The mountain man stared at his coffee. He just wanted to be outside, but living far back in the mountains meant he had to ride out many storms.

His enormous beard wiggled. "What little critter got in there now?" he wondered.

His attention went to the dripping water from a roof leak. He thought, "I knew I should have waited out this storm in the old motorhome."

He heard something hit the side of the shack. "Did the wind hurl a pinecone or was it them slapping the wall to see if he was okay?" he wondered. He punched the inside wall. A slap from the outside answered. He smiled.

The next morning, clouds still raced across a blue sky backdrop. All the vegetation was wet and the ground moist. As the temperature increased, so did the humidity. The warm, damp conditions made me feel like I was in a sauna as we hiked toward the mountain cabin.

"Do you think he will remember us?" asked my friend and fellow Bigfoot investigator.

"Yes, I bet he will. Look for hair samples, that sample I got last year was from his beard. There has to be Bigfoot hair around there!" I exclaimed. "His shack should be just around the next corner."

"Hello," I said but, he was outside and saw us immediately. "We met you last summer after hiking here from the National Forest! How are you?"

"Yeah, yous are interested in da Bigfoot."

"We are," I said. "We brought you a Bigfoot coffee mug, a camo beanie with a bear silhouette on it and a gift certificate to the hardware store down in town. The beanie is for when you want a break from wearing your skunk fur hat – not replace it – I'm sure you would replace it with another skunk – well, anyway, we hope you like these."

He was ready to decline the gifts but he thought about his leaky roof and would need some supplies from town to fix it properly. With the gift certificate to the hardware store he would be able to purchase the much needed supplies. "Well, that is very kind of ya."

"We were hoping to stay on your property tonight." I paused, waiting to hear banjo music. "Is that okay with you?"

"I have never allowed any hunting or such stuff here," he answered. "But, yous seem to have a respect for the forest. Need to camp right over there near the border of the National Forest," he pointed.

"Thank you very much! Have you seen that mountain lion with ten inch fangs again?"

"I have," he said staring at us to observe our reaction. "Ya be careful!"

"Oh great!" I thought. "He is still seeing saber-toothed tigers!"

We went to the observation spot. "This is not the most ideal location. We can't see the tree that has all those deer, elk and moose antlers. Did you see the pile of antlers at the base of the tree?" I asked my friend. "Those were not there last year. Bigfoot continues to gift him antlers."

"A Bigfoot could approach the tree and we would not see it with our thermal imagers because the motorhome is blocking us," he said. "Another thing, we are downwind from the outhouse."

We were behind a huge fir that had apparently blown down in the storm last night. We were protected from any wind but, it would still be cold at night. As the temperature dropped, we began stuffing hand warmers in every pocket.

"I hope we brought enough warm clothes," I shivered. "We better record a bigfoot on our thermals!"

"The problem is, if we record one, it will probably be peeking around the shack and the public will just say it was the mountain man!" my friend stated.

"I agree. Hopefully, we will record an entire body showing the same heat pattern all over. Then we can compare that to a person with a jacket on. It will not convince everyone. I don't care what others think. It will prove it to us, as we are here experiencing it. This will be interesting – I'm sure the Bigfoot heard our voices and know we are here. We may not see anything."

It got colder than a well digger's arse. We thought about leaving in the dark with our headlamps, but we stuck it out.

In my slumber, I felt the rising sun on my face. But, a shadow blocked the sun and I awoke. In front of me was a tall, dark, upright figure. It was dark because the sun was behind it. "Bigfoot!" I thought. I gasped. My friend gasped as he awoke.

"Yous boys see anything?" the mountain man asked. He was wearing the camo beanie and it made his head, with the sun behind it, look similar to most Bigfoot.

"Uh, no," I replied.

"Good, I was worried that mountain lion might git ya. Well, I'll see yous next summer. Another beanie would be nice. This one smells better than my skunk fur hat!"

Great Lengths

From the title of this chapter, you may think it is about measuring footprints, distance between Bigfoot tracks, estimating height of a seen Bigfoot, etc. But, it actually brings to light the great lengths we go to in pursuit of this mystery. One example is the discussion that took place while camping in one remote site.

The only way to get into the suspected area of Bigfoot activity was to cross a cold mountain stream.

"We can cross now by stepping on exposed rocks," I said. "But, if we come back here earlier next year, the water level will be higher. The increased water depth and speed of flow will make it too dangerous to cross. Bigfoot is over there for a reason – they know people cannot easily hike into that area."

That prompted hours of discussion on techniques to safely cross the rocky stream.

One Bigfoot investigator said, "We can tie a rope to trees that are across from each other, then hold onto it as we wade across."

"I can take the rope across in a raft," I added.

"Or a kayak," someone said. "But, I think the current will be too fast."

Someone else had the idea, "We can put up a zip line!"

"Build sections of small docks and they can be removed when we leave," was another idea. It was overly discussed until we had the exact amount of two by fours needed and approximate cost to build.

"A rope swing won't make it across."

"A few extension ladders tied end to end and laid down to walk on would reach across," someone brainstormed.

"And best to lay boards over the rungs," I added. "I think that is the best option! Maybe we should all wear helmets in case someone falls off - or we will just wait for Bigfoot to cross the stream and come to us."

A Second Letter To Bigfoot, from Kevin's Wife

Dear Bigfoot,

In my first letter, I listed inconveniences you have caused over the years. I hope you gave them serious consideration.

But, there have been positives that have come from the amount of time Kevin has spent camping and looking for you. I guess I should give you a little credit for these positives that have come from his passion for you.

For example, because Kevin returns home with scratches, scrapes, bug bites and stings, I bought stock in companies making bandages, sting relief products and triple antibiotic ointment. These stocks are doing very well. The increase in value of these stocks seem to coincide with the increase in Kevin's age.

These camping/scouting trips for Bigfoot do prevent boredom and increase laughter and smiles – not only for Kevin, but the stories he recounts upon his return, make me smile.

Kevin occasionally does oil painting. When he comes home, he is inspired to paint more nature scenes with a Bigfoot included.

He disconnects from Wi-Fi and connects with nature.

Kevin may come home exhausted, but these regular trips to the mountains result in increased exercise. More exercise is always a positive, even if acetaminophen is taken before, during and after a hike. I will be buying stock in acetaminophen next!

He has increased his survival skills. He is always prepared but a person has to be aware of the perils of nature at all times.

As a result of chasing you, Kevin has increased his knowledge about plants and other animals. Because he is a veterinarian, he is mostly interested in animal behaviors and how they live. He still needs to learn more about plants. So, I hope he doesn't eat some dangerous plant by mistake.

When in the forest, Kevin is looking for signs other animals leave and you leave an occasional track, just to tease. So, he is constantly improving as a tracker. His wandering looking for you has lead him into many forests. He has discovered amazing places he would not have found otherwise.

When camping Kevin has learned to look up. We do not look up enough in life to admire the majesty of nature. Look up during the day to see a hawk soaring above a mountain. Look up to see the sun rise and set. Look up at night to see the stars. Both of us agree – this makes a person feel small in comparison. This makes Kevin realize there are so many things to be discovered and many mysteries remain around us.

At the top of the list of positives is the friends he has made over all these years. I know he cherishes connecting with like-minded people. People that share the passion for the topic of Bigfoot.

Bigfoot, in my opinion it is fine for you to remain a mystery. However, Kevin loves the mystery so continue your hide and seek lifestyle.

Maybe, I can overlook a few things; all the scratches on his pickup, too much camping equipment, money spent on thermal imagers, cameras and audio recorders, etc. But, I am worried because he is loading extension ladders in his truck. I may have misunderstood, but he said he is using them to walk across a stream!

Signed,
Kevin's wife

Bull

It is wonderful to hear birds when I'm in the forest, except when they wake me up when I am trying to sleep in after a long night of listening for Bigfoot vocalizations.

I was half-asleep because the birds had been singing and tweeting since just before first light. I was trying to ignore them and get some more sleep. The flap over my tent window was down. I had that feeling of being watched. I looked out the tent window into the increasing daylight. There was a black face looking back at me. The dark eyes were round, huge, staring, but with a curious look. The nose was large and moist. The lips were wide. The large ears moved back and forth. Ears??? I bet you thought I was describing a Bigfoot face looking into my tent! It was a bull.

Livestock grazing permits can be obtained for some national forests. Many places in the Pacific Northwest have cattle roaming the forests during the summer. They stand in the middle of the Forest Service road and won't move. They stare at you with that curious, yet dumb look. They leave "cow pies" in the meadows where I want to pitch my tent and on some trails. Between cattle, moose, bear, deer and elk manure on some trails – I won't describe the state of my boots.

Some of the "cow pies" in the road end up coating the wheel wells of my truck. This mixes with the mud and dust already there. Maybe Bigfoot cannot smell my old, oily truck coming due to this.

Besides the manure, a Bigfoot investigator has to be aware of the presence of cattle. Once, my dad and I were riding our trail motorcycles in the mountains. The road narrowed and had thick, tall brush on each side. I was in the lead and suddenly this black face thrust from the brush and jutted into the road in front of me. I thought I was going to broadside a black bear that was about to step in front of me. I almost "laid the bike down." It was a bull, not a bear. Later, my dad laughed and laughed.

Another time, I was fishing a remote stream in my float tube. I was standing in my float tube in hip deep water. I was on the edge casting into a corner of the stream. Across the stream, was a large sandbar that followed the curve of the stream to my left. I planned to check the sand for tracks after I finished casting into the fishing hole in front of me. The brush was thick and maybe seven feet tall behind the sandbar. I heard the crashing and saw the tops of the brush wave back and forth as something was walking toward the sandbar. "It has to be a Bigfoot pushing its way through the brush," I thought. "It does not know I'm across the stream and I will have a great, close sighting!" A huge bull walked onto the sandbar.

So, when it comes to Bigfooting, grab the bull by the horns. Put one's hand to the plow. The proof of Bigfoot is at "steak." This story is "udderly" done before you have a "beef" with the puns.

Part Two
Rocking BF Ranch

Wild Men

The bough of the giant fir hung in front of the cowboy's face. It did not totally block his view of the high mountain meadow as he sat his saddle. The bough barely moved as a light breeze landed on his face. Francis was downwind, just the way he wanted. He arrived at dawn and did not want to risk being seen by crossing the huge meadow so he held up by the giant fir. Beyond the meadow were magnificent rock formations that reached high into the sky. His partner, Ben, had remained at camp to watch the cattle.

The bough turned golden as the first rays of sunshine came through the trees at sunrise. The mule deer feeding in the middle of the meadow turned golden tan in the sun. The cowboy's young, sharp eyes scanned the far tree line for any movement. Strange, he did not hear any birds. He should have been hearing them fill the air with early morning song.

Suddenly, the deer's head shot up and stared at the far side of the meadow. It bounded off as if its legs were on springs. The cowboy spotted an upright figure moving just inside the far tree line. He removed the leather hammer thong that held his revolver in its holster. He slightly pulled up the .44 Colt just to make sure it would come out of the holster as fast as possible. His lever action rifle was in the scabbard.

"I knew you would come to this area," he thought. He had left camp long before dawn. There was no trail to follow, he just had a hunch to investigate this mountain meadow. After what he saw in the campfire light the night before, he knew he must see it again to confirm it was real.

The night before at camp, they had cooked venison and ate huckleberries for dessert. The smell of the fried deer meat had lingered in the cool mountain air. The carcass of the deer was far from camp hanging high in a tree to reduce the chance of a bear getting it. It was cool in a grove of trees next to the creek that flowed with icy water from the mountains above.

It was dark with a crescent moon rising in the sky. It provided just enough light to see white faces of the cattle and observe the calmness of the herd.

Francis pulled a harmonica from his shirt pocket. Ben smiled as he knew the nightly ritual was about to be repeated: for entertainment and to soothe the cattle. After playing a soothing song, the cowboy opened his eyes and could not believe what he saw. It was peeking around a nearby tree. It had long hair hanging from the head and shoulders but did not cover the flat face. The large eyes glowed red in the light of the campfire. A long arm hung by its side. He had never seen nor heard of anything like this living in the mountains. Francis was young and new to this part of the country. He was in disbelief and time seemed to stand still. He could not ask his friend if he was seeing it. The figure then moved behind the tree and was gone.

"Well, Francis, are you done playing?" Ben asked.

"Did you see that?" Francis demanded.

"No, what is there?" Ben asked while grabbing the handle of his revolver.

"It – it must have been a bear."

"I hope it doesn't climb the tree and get our deer. I was counting on venison for the next several days," Ben announced.

Francis was still staring at the tree.

"Do you want to take first watch?" Ben asked as he put his head back on his saddle and tipped his hat down over his eyes.

"Yeah, I'll take first watch." The young cowboy knew he could not sleep anyway. He replayed the sighting over and over in his mind and barely heard his friend snoring.

––––––––––––––––––

Francis moved his horse forward into the meadow. Once, he looked down and saw a huge footprint. The back half had crushed the grass but the front half landed in the soft dirt of a ground squirrel mound. Five toes showed clearly in the early morning sun. He slowly and quietly moved across the large opening.

The trees on the far side were sparser. He moved forward, hoping his horse would alert him to any danger. Sure enough, the horse stopped suddenly with ears erect. What Francis did next, he had done a million times before. In a split second his lever action rifle came out of the scabbard, to his shoulder and the iron sights were on target. But then he remembered the eyes and face from last night.

What was it? A wild man? It was early in the twentieth century and the name Bigfoot would not be coined until 1958. The creature made long strides with arms swinging and disappeared into the huge boulders at the base of the rock formations.

Arriving back at camp, he saw Ben on the ground propped up against his saddle. He had cut a slit up the left side of his pants to expose a huge swelling of his lower leg with a lot of bruising.

"How did you hurt your leg?"

"After sunrise, I went to check on our deer. It's gone! If something had chewed on it, there should be a few scraps on the ground. Nothing there at all. Not even any drag mark on the ground. When I got back here, a rock the size of a calf's head came flying from those trees." He pointed to the tree where the creature had been watching camp the previous night. "And what is with you? What did you see in those trees? Since then you have become an odd stick, Francis." Francis could not tell his friend and partner in the cattle business what he had seen even though they had been friends since five years of age.

"You know me, I'm just a wild man. Can you ride?"

"If you help me saddle up my horse and get me in the saddle."

"I think there are too many bears around following the ripening huckleberries. Let's move the cattle lower. There is still enough green grass down there. We can always come back here in a month. In his mind, Francis actually wanted to come back and see the wild men and play his harmonica for them. He wanted to have them around, through time.

Tales from the Squatters

Francis was sitting on the porch enthralled by the fall colors. The ranch house, which had come along nicely over the last few years, was in the valley and their land extended high into the mountains. Looking out across the ranch, he thought the trees appeared painted. He knew he should go inside, start a fire in the stove and cook some grub. The chill in the air meant this would probably be the first night for a fire in the fireplace. But, he was transfixed on the fall colors and appreciation of what he and Ben were building. It had been a lot of hard work but he reminded himself it all started with luck. They had set out as teenagers. During their travels, they had stopped in what is now the upper section of their ranch. They found gold – not a lot, but they immediately filed for ownership of the land.

Ben was supposed to be back today from a hunting trip into the high country but the sun was getting low in the sky. Francis knew Ben would be hungry upon his return and appreciate some hot food. Ben entered the ranch house just as the beef stew was hot and ready.

"Hey Ben, did you get an elk?" Francis greeted his friend and business partner.

"I quickly got one and would have been back yesterday but, we have a problem. We have squatters in the upper land!"

"What! How many? Did you tell them they are on our ranch, the Rocking BF?"

"I told them. I talked to them all day yesterday. It is just one family. They have not been there long."

"That is crazy!" Francis exclaimed. "It will start snowing up there any day!"

"I told them that and the hut they quickly erected would not provide any protection from the upcoming wind and temperatures. They are greenhorns – as green as the spring grass. They realized they need to go to town and find jobs for the winter. But, they are also leaving for other reasons."

"What other reasons?" Francis asked.

"After I wolf down some stew, I have the wildest tales from the squatters to share," Ben said staring at the stew.

Enjoying the warmth of the fireplace, Ben began with the details he got from the squatters.

"The first night they were in the hut, they began to smell the most rotten odor. The wife described it as skunk but the husband as a rotting animal. Later, things began to hit the walls of the shanty. In the morning, they found sticks, pinecones and rocks outside the shanty. No rotting animal was found nearby as the source of the odor."

"What is going on up there, Francis? What throws pinecones and rocks? Remember a few years ago, my leg was hit with a rock and it hurt for days!"

"How can I forget? You bring it up often enough!" Francis mumbled. "I don't know how to explain it. Could have been the wind blowing pinecones off the trees but, rocks being thrown!" Francis wondered if this was the time to tell Ben about the wild men. Francis had wanted more interaction with the creatures. Over the last few years, he would make excuses to Ben so he could spend a night in the upper meadows. Excuses such as; checking for strays, checking for wolves, observing where the elk were hanging out and searching for a place to build a hunting cabin. When he would go there, he would occasionally get glimpses of the upright wild creatures. He would play the harmonica at dusk and hear knocks on wood similar to someone chopping wood but he knew it was not that. Francis never felt he was in danger from them.

Ben continued, "A couple mornings later, the squatters stepped out of the hut to find two logs, each about ten feet long laying on the ground in the shape of an X. On each side of the X was a stack of rocks. Now, explain that, Francis!"

"Interesting! Could a bear have rolled the logs off the hill above?"

"But, what can stack and throw rocks?" Ben almost shouted. "They also felt they were being watched all the time. They heard blood curdling screams, whistles and what sounded like people talking in the distance. This was in the middle of the night – the night before I talked to them! So, they want to leave! I told them to be aware of mountain lions and pointed them in the direction of town."

Francis pondered, "I hope they don't tell the town folks. People may come up here out of curiosity." Francis did not want trespassers harassing the wild men.

"I think they were scared and in disbelief. They may blame us as the answer to all those occurrences. Especially after I showed up. They may think I was the one screaming. I figured it was mountain lions. I hope they don't tell people

I was talking to myself!" Ben was embarrassed at that thought.

"Yeah, between the wind, bear, mountain lions, owls and all the critters up there, I think their imaginations got the best of them. That's what we will say if any town folk start spreading rumors."

Ben raised his voice, "But, what throws and stacks rocks?"

"You must be tired, Ben. Time for some shut-eye."

Music – The Universal Language

Francis stopped his horse in the shade and watched the cattle drink from the creek. The day had been hot and dusty. He rode upstream where no cattle were mudding the stream. He dismounted, dunked his head in the cool water and rinsed his sweaty hat. He saw his reflection in a small pool of still water. A leathery, somber face appeared in the water. It had been a rough way to make a living but he would not have had it any other way. He would rather be in the saddle, not sitting on a porch in some town. He heard a large branch break and he smiled.

After making a small campfire for the night and eating some venison jerky, he began memorializing about his friend and business partner, Ben. The perils of nature had cut his life short. The old cowboy missed him. He thought about the time the wild men of the mountains had hit his friend's leg with a rock. That occurred near this very spot. He was sure the wild men did not mean to hit Ben – just wanted to let him know he was in their territory. His friend did not understand what in the forest could throw a rock. He talked about it often.

"What do you think could do that?" Ben would always ask. "Did you see anybody on the mountain that morning? Heck, we were the only people to ever go up there."

The old cowboy never told Ben that he had seen a big hairy creature with long arms.

His memories were interrupted by whoops coming from the trees above. His horse snorted. It was dusk and time to pull out the harmonica. The wild men knew this and the whoops were their request for music.

Wild men? A few years ago, the old cowboy had seen a newspaper when he was in town for supplies. There was an article about Bigfoot in another part of the country. So, that's what they are calling them! Someone had made a plaster cast of a track.

"Why would you want to make a cast of a track?" he thought. "I see their tracks every day!" Another whoop broke the silence.

He did not consider himself a musician, in that he would never play in town at a community dance. He had played all his life. He didn't care if he was not a great musician and apparently the

Bigfoot didn't either. Another whoop came from a different location.

He finally started to play. He chose some songs his friend had liked. After each song, wood knocks rang out as if applauding. It made the old cowboy smile. He had Bigfoot around his camps throughout his time on the ranch. He reminisced about some of those encounters. The old cowboy thought of them as a part of nature. If his friend was still around, he would be a knower about Bigfoot. Another whoop interrupted his memories again.

He held the harmonica in his leathery hands. It was his connection to Bigfoot. Music is the universal language throughout time.

The Special Ranch

James, Ben's son, looked down on the ranch house his dad and Francis had built. He watched people leaving. He stood among the headstones of his mom, Ben and Francis. The memorial for Francis had just ended.

He held a small wooden box Francis had left for him. His fingers moved over the carving in the lid. It was a carving of a person walking. But, was it a person? It had a large round head, large feet and the length of the arms seemed exaggerated.

He opened the box and inside was a harmonica and a letter. He unfolded the letter and began to read.

Dear James,

Unfortunately, your dad passed when you were only a few years old. You never got to experience what a great man he was. Do you even remember living here? Your mom, being a school teacher, naturally wanted to live in town rather than here in the mountains. So, after Ben passed, she moved out of here. I tried to visit with you when I occasionally would go to town.

I know you have a successful business in town. You have declined my offer of partnership in the ranch multiple times over the years. But, it is yours now. I hope and pray you will sell your business in town and move your family here. Your roots are here. With that new automobile you have, you can be in town in no time at all and enjoy both worlds.

It is a special ranch. I do mean special. I have never told another soul about this including your father. However, he had his suspicions about what is here. I have shared the land with some other people. Well, I have always called them wild men. But, I have also seen tracks that can only be their young. A few years ago, I read in a newspaper they were calling them Bigfoot in another part of the country. They probably have been here on this land since the beginning of time, I don't know.

Take the harmonica and ride to the upper meadows at the base of the rock formations. At dusk, play or practice playing the harmonica. Don't be afraid. They will become used to you. Just let them do what they want.

I know this is hard to believe. You know I was never loco. This is my last request, that you give this special place a chance and don't sell it.

With love,

Francis

James was bewildered, yet curious. That evening, he was in the area Francis had written about. After what he saw that night, he could never sell the ranch. He would continue to learn about Bigfoot for the rest of his time and, as his son grew up, they would share many experiences with Bigfoot.

Difficult Choice

Hard times can come to any business and this year the Rocking BF had been hit with a whirlwind of difficulties. A couple were huge. The first to raise its sickening head was a disease storm that went through the herd that spring. There was a lack of spring rains followed by very hot temperatures and the ranch became a tinder box. When a fire broke out in the barn, it destroyed the huge structure and sparked a wildfire that burned a lot of valuable timber and grassland.

James and his son Daniel sat on the porch of the ranch house, both in a somber mood. They could smell the pile of charred wood that used to be the barn. James was depressed about the financial state of the ranch. Daniel would turn twenty one this fall but how could any of them feel like celebrating?

"Dad, that contagious disease has caused us to depopulate the herd. The veterinarian has been here a ton and his bills are due. He said the disease most likely came from elk. So, he needs to treat all the cattle – the few remaining head and all new ones. Please tell me, can the ranch survive? How many calving seasons will it take to recover?"

"I don't know, son. It's an understatement that we have been hit with bad luck. That is why I have been looking for gold in the upper streams. Remember the ranch history? Your grandfather and his best friend Francis, found some gold up there. Enough to lay claim to this land and water. They bought some cattle that would turn into a large herd. I have found only a few flakes, so that is why I brought in a geologist the other day."

"A geologist? To do what?" asked Daniel.

"To help find gold. There is a lot of Quartz up there and some gold has been found in the streams coming out of the rock formations. Over time, gold may be washing out of those jutting formations. There is no guarantee, but those are good indicators of more gold to be found. They would set up in that huge meadow. They would drill, tunnel toward the rock formations and do some blasting into them."

"No, dad! That is where the Bigfoot live, or at least hang out most of the year. Tunneling? Blasting? That would destroy their home!"

James shook his head. "Mining gold would solve our financial problems and save the ranch."

"This ranch is the Rocking BF. Sometimes I think the BF stands for Bigfoot because they have been here forever."

James needed to calm his son down. "You know BF are the initials of their first names. Francis was the one who interacted with them for many years and he only called them Bigfoot shortly before passing. But, to let you know, I am sick about making the choice between mining or leaving the Bigfoot in peace with the chance of risking the ranch."

"Dad, you know I don't want to go anywhere. I want to remain on this ranch all my life and I want Bigfoot to be a part of the ranch, always. I'm going to camp up there for a couple days." Daniel left in a huff.

James let out a long sigh. His stomach hurt.

Three days had passed and James was getting worried about Daniel. Mining for gold would assure the passing of the ranch to Daniel. But, the Bigfoot seemed to accept Daniel and the interactions between them were amazing. Time after time, James started to pick up the phone to call the geologist and arrange a meeting with the mining outfit but he never followed through.

Daniel burst into the house and threw his backpack on the table. His hands were shaking as he unzipped it.

"Dad! You won't believe it! I was sitting by one of the creek pools, depressed and staring at the water. A ray of sun came through the trees and I saw something shiny in the bottom of the pool. Look what I found!"

Daniel reached in the backpack and pulled out a chunk of gold the size of a baseball. He then pulled out handfuls of pea sized nuggets.

"I spent my time digging in the stream pools. We don't have to tunnel or blast, just expand and dig the pools deeper. We should find gold and it will create better water holding areas for the cattle. That's what is needed during dry summers. Water will still run down here to the lower elevations, too. There may be a vein of gold up there but all we need is enough to secure the ranch which will protect the Bigfoot!"

"I know your birthday is three months off, but happy twenty first, son!"

Happy One Hundredth

Brittany burst into the ranch house frantically yelling for her sister. She was in such a panic she did not know where to begin to look for Danielle.

"Danielle! Danielle, come quick! Dad is injured outside!"

Danielle came running from the new addition to the ranch house. "I was checking on Grandpa James, what is the matter?"

"Dad is outside, injured. He is still on his horse. Come help!" Brittany said as she ran for the door.

Danielle was the older sister. She had a strong personality and always said what was on her mind. She was basically running the Rocking BF ranch in her mid-twenties. Daniel was draped over his saddle.

"What did you do, Dad?"

"I fell out of the tree stand," Daniel groaned. "I think both my hips are broken."

"You were looking for trespassers again from tree stands, weren't you?" Danielle said in frustration. "How did you get on your horse?

They helped you, didn't they? The Bigfoot helped you! That just takes the cake – tomorrow we were going to celebrate the one hundredth year of the Rocking BF, but Bigfoot and you take center stage!"

"Get me to the hospital!" Daniel shouted. A ranch hand came running from the barn to help.

Before Daniel was discharged after bilateral hip replacement surgery the sheriff, Roy, stopped by to visit. They had been friends since high school.

"Hello, Mr. Tin Badge!" Daniel teased. "Thanks for checking in on me."

"I heard you fell out of a tree stand – that was real smart of you! You must be getting dumber with age," Roy quipped back. "You still having problems with trespassers?"

"I told you last year I saw some people up in the rock formations. Well, this spring I found two trail cameras up there. I backtracked the trespassers and discovered a narrow passage in the rock formation that leads to the national forest beyond. How anybody found it in those rugged formations is beyond me. That passage is the only way to walk onto the ranch from that direction. If it weren't for the steep terrain of the backside of the ranch, I probably would have more trespassers."

"After your report last summer, I talked to a couple Forest Service Rangers. They told me to keep it to myself, but they had two separate reports of backpackers being chased by Bigfoot. Both times, the people were near the backside of the Rocking BF. It is a long way from the nearest campground to your property through rugged terrain. But, a few people will hike it."

"Bigfoot! Are they sure they had Bigfoot chasing them and not bear?"

"They reported Bigfoot. That is just between you and me. But, Daniel, what have you really experienced up there? You've never said anything to me but over the years, the rumors have persisted that the Rocking BF is a hotspot for Bigfoot."

Daniel stared out the hospital window and didn't respond.

"You know, even people with a passing interest in Bigfoot make note of road crossings and other sightings in the area. Other people mark encounters on maps and put them on social media," Roy stated.

"Social media has ruined everything!" Daniel announced.

Daniel's recovery went well, his two doting daughters and wife made sure! In fact, he needed to get away for a day ride – to check the narrow passage.

It felt good to be on his horse again. He often imagined Ben and Francis riding there for the first time one hundred years ago with Bigfoot watching them. He kept an eye out for new trail cameras. He dismounted near the narrow passage and entered it on foot. We was astonished by what he saw half way down the passage. The passage was blocked with large boulders and logs all jammed together.

"How did this happen?" his brain just had to ask. But, he knew. "Well, Bigfoot has stopped the trespassers. I'm sure the Bigfoot can still probably move over to the national forest if they want. They would know how to do it. I'm sure they want to stay on the ranch undisturbed."

Starting back late in the day, he entered the huge meadow. A ground squirrel dove off its dirt mound making an alarm call as it disappeared into its burrow. A wood knock rang out. It was answered from another location. Another knock came from a third location.

Smiling, he stopped and turned his horse. He looked at the magnificent scenery.

"Happy one hundredth Rocking BF Ranch!"

Part Three
Final Thoughts

Huckleberry Patches

Huckleberries are prevalent throughout Northeast Washington and North Idaho and my family has many delicious recipes for the precious little berry. Precious, in that it takes time to pick just one quart. But, the thought of eating huckleberry pie makes me pick faster! When a great patch loaded with large berries is found, the location is kept to yourself. Before our wedding, I told my wife I wanted it in our vows that she will not reveal locations of huckleberry patches (just kidding!)

Because they are so valuable, you do not want to trip and fall, spilling your bucket. Or, the other unfortunate situation I have experienced is stepping on top of an underground hornet's nest. Running through the forest wildly waving my arms is not conducive to keeping a full bucket of berries.

Huckleberry patches not only attract people but many other animals. It has never happened to me, but I have talked to many people that have been run out of a berry patch by bear. I am sure

Bigfoot is attracted to this food source also. Not only is the berry something to eat but do Bigfoot watch for other animals attracted to the berries and consider some of them a food source? It would make sense Bigfoot would watch these areas. The only times I felt as if I was being watched in the forest have been while picking huckleberries.

I could discuss the many stories about Bigfoot and its odor, but those stories would stink (pun intended.)

I believe that most times I have smelled a foul odor, it was elk. But, one time while picking huckleberries, there was a series of events which odor was just a part of.

It was a sunny, warm day without a breeze. I had the feeling of being watched. While in the berry patch, I kept looking north into the trees. I heard whoops to the northeast. I immediately began trying to rule out Raven or any other animal. Then, there was the sound of a branch break to the north. I heard walking that sure sounded like bipedal steps. I was on my knees staring toward these close sounds. My hands and fingers continued moving in a picking fashion but were grabbing nothing while I focused into the trees. Then I smelled a manure-like odor that dissipated after several minutes. I did not move. I did not see anything. Was it an elk? But, elk do not do wood knocks. When I got back to the pickup, a wood knock rang out to the northeast. Another answered from the northwest. The pattern repeated three more times. Hmmm…..

When an encounter occurs, I hope there will be two or more Bigfoot related activities, different vocalizations or findings. Then I can say to a skeptic, "Can you explain that to me! Can you give me an explanation that it was something other than Bigfoot. Sometimes, it can be nothing but Bigfoot."

Every animal needs food, water and cover. Bigfoot is no different. When in the forest, I pay close attention to the location of fresh animal tracks and why they are there at that time of year. If Bigfoot is in the region, they may be in that area for the same reasons.

Let's Face It

Five of us were packed into the small SUV scouting the mountain roads looking for animal tracks on the banks of the roads. Both the scenery and the weather were beautiful. A crystal clear mountain stream was a moderate distance below us on our left. I was still getting to know the lead investigator that was driving. He stopped suddenly and pointed to the sandbar on our side of the stream.

"It looks like possibly a large Bigfoot track there on the sandbar!" he exclaimed. "I want to look at it through the binoculars."

We stood on the edge of the road and after we looked through the binoculars, all of us agreed it appeared to be a footprint. But the hillside dropped off from the toes of our boots at a very steep angle.

"We can't get down there to check it out," someone stated.

"Yes we can," I said. "We can drop down to that huge cedar tree and then switchback along the hillside down to the sandbar. Follow me."

I followed my predetermined route and made it safely down to the sandbar. I thought everyone was behind me but when I looked up toward the road, there were four faces staring over the edge at me.

"I thought all of you were coming with me? What are you still doing up there?" I yelled.

"You did great!" someone yelled back. "Now go look at the track!"

I will never forget those four faces peering back at me. Because they were some distance away, I could not tell if they were smirking at me or in awe that I traversed such terrain. Was this an initiation of some sort into the group of serious Bigfooters? Were they observing what lengths I would actually go to in investigating something possibly Bigfoot related? No, I was just proud of the safe execution of my plan. I actually began to chuckle because I figured I was braver than them.

"There is no footprint here!" I yelled.

"Yes there is, right in front of you," was the response.

"No! No Bigfoot track nor any other track here." We were seeing a pattern that was not a footprint. It was just the way the light was angled on the sand and river rock.

My fellow investigators did not need to lower a rope to pull me up from the sandbar. I made it back to the road. I only slid backwards downhill once!

Pareidolia is when one sees a pattern or object where there is none. Faces are very often seen in shadows, rock formations, etc. I have read studies about pareidolia and would encourage everyone to do the same. Our minds are conditioned to see faces from infancy. We have needed to see faces through time to socially recognize friends, foes and identify predators.

One time in the mountains, I looked across the canyon at a rock formation that looked like a giant face in agony. The setting sun on it highlighted the evil looking "eyes" and "mouth." It was creepy. I took several pictures with my digital camera. I showed them on my camera to my fellow investigator later. What was even creepier is when I got home, those pictures were not on the memory card. The other pictures from the trip were.

Back to the topic of pareidolia. Let's face it, still pictures of shadows in the forest and rock formations lead often to seeing faces and patterns that are not there. If we would have taken a picture from the road of what we thought was a footprint on the sandbar and shared with others, people would probably see a Bigfoot track. But, it was not there. Upon investigating, it was proven to be pareidolia.

I remind myself constantly, if I think Bigfoot is possibly near, press the record button to get video. It is better to record movement and analyze that, than to have a still picture that shows a face or pattern of a body part that is not there. We need to see movement. Photos of shadows and/or blurry expanded pictures of shadows in the bushes prove nothing and only give skeptics reasons to dismiss the topic of Bigfoot.

Vague Answers

We had the border agent surrounded – well, not really. But, my family was talking to him through both windows of his pickup. He was very engaging, funny and a delight to converse with. We were in Washington State, near the Canadian border. He had stopped at our camp to give us the "be bear aware" discourse because three weeks before, he saw a grizzly sow and her two cubs at our camp location.

He was entertaining all of us with brief stories from on-the-job experiences.

"This is my chance to ask him if he has seen Bigfoot," I thought. But, what would be his response? Would he laugh? Would he just ignore the question?

"Have you ever seen a Bigfoot?" I asked.

"That would be something!" he replied. "This would be the place to see one."

That triggered my memories of all the vocalizations, encounters and possible Bigfoot tracks I had heard and found in this area over the years. Especially that track I suspicioned was Bigfoot and not bear. It was on the edge of the logging road, but an ATV tire had rolled over the back half. I had casting material with me and it would have definitely been a track to cast, if not ruined by tire tread. Sometimes, bad luck is a huge part of Bigfooting. My thoughts were brought back to the present by what the agent said next.

"Sometimes our horses get spooked. Last summer, we had an agent bucked off his horse and had to be air lifted out of here."

"We were camped here when that happened," my sister said. "The helicopter landed right over there in that open area."

"Wait!" I thought. "Did he just say an agent's horse was spooked by a Bigfoot and threw the rider?" He worded that vaguely. He did not actually say a Bigfoot was seen or responsible for spooking the horse – but was he implying Bigfoot was involved?

"Well, I need to get going," he said. "You folks have fun camping!"

"Wait!" I thought. "I want to hear more!"

This is how things stand when it comes to talking about Bigfoot. Vague answers, or no answers at all are given because someone is afraid of ridicule. They do not want to admit they saw one or are in disbelief. Details are forgotten or not shared. Details about appearance and behavior that would help add more pieces to the puzzle – the puzzle of solving this mystery. The details are important. If possible, focus on the details of every encounter. Let's continue to cast possible tracks, collect hair samples, get video and other evidence. Let's keep it real and progress will continue to complete the puzzle.

Many questions remain. In my first book, **Incessantly Bigfooting,** I mentioned when I was a youngster I became a member of Roger Patterson's Northwest Research Association. He mailed bulletins (newsletters) to the members. I quote from Bulletin No. 4

"There are a lot of questions unanswered but as research goes on we will eventually have all of those answers."

Continue incessantly Bigfooting.

Bigfoot Poem

My quest for you has been long,
I have left gifts and often played you a song.
I have investigated with respect and passion,
But at times you made my face go ashen.
I have continued to go with the flow,
Because I don't just believe - I know.

Into the woods we headed for a stint,
Only to find a giant footprint.
It was not bear or cougar,
I need to get a longer ruler.
I know what made this thing,
In the woods it is king.

There I was far from home,
Just went to explore and roam.
The thunder sounded with a crack,
A wood knock answered with a whack.
Then the lightning lit up the woods,
Tall and hairy there you stood.

There was a connection when our eyes met,
My brain did a reset.
I did not feel a threat,
Neither of us were upset.
The memory you left me with,
I know you are no myth.

I know you see us all the time,
When we see you that's big time.
Some say when we see you that's by design,
Some say we have had too much moonshine.
I know what I have seen and heard - it's sublime,
Can't wait til again it is showtime.

Bigfooting Glossary

There are words and phrases that are unique to certain parts of the country. This is true for the Pacific Northwest. For example, "The mountain is out" means it is a clear day and Mt. Rainier can be seen for miles. "In the sticks" means you are in a remote area.

The following is my general list of some words and phrases relating to the outdoors and Bigfooting.

Air mattress: always flat by morning.

Ape: Bigfoot does not want to be called this.

Bear: the culprit that often leaves a "double step" track that looks similar to a Bigfoot track.

Boulder: something to hide behind when humans approach.

Camera: remember to take the lens cover off.

Campfire: stress reliever.

Cascade pinstriping: scratches on your vehicle after exploring for Bigfoot in the Cascade Mountains of Washington.

Cast: sure to break while digging it out.

Cave: Bigfoot's home? But, I'm not going in to find out!

Coyote: Bigfoot hangs with them because they know where the rabbits are.

Deadfall: always blocking my path – something I trip over instead of taking two minutes to walk around.

Did you hear that: the four most spoken words in the forest.

Drone: piece of equipment to crash into a tree.

Equipment: items to completely fill a basement.

First aid kit: must have.

Gibberish/Chatter: language understood by Bigfoot.

GPS: don't trust when says "turn right now" and you are on the edge of a drop-off.

Headlamp: red or white, that is the question.

Howl: when Bigfoot drops a rock on his big toe.

Lake: Bigfoot's bathtub.

Mountain: favorite place to be for me and Bigfoot.

Multi-tool: self-defining. Don't leave home without one.

Odor: time to go to the lake!

Rocks: playthings for Bigfoot – make nice clacking sounds and throws like a baseball.

Spork: Lusikkahaarukka is Finnish for spoon-fork combination.

Scouting: fastest way to put scratches and dents on your truck.

Sunset: time to get ready for nighttime Bigfoot activity.

Tarp: becomes a large kite in the wind.

Technology: expensive toys for me to play with.

Tent: has zippers that Bigfoot likes to play with.

Tracks: left by Bigfoot just to tease humans.

Trail: a mountain path that is usually too steep for me.

Trail camera: be careful what you do in the woods, cameras are everywhere

Truck: never has enough room for all my stuff to go to "the sticks."

Turkey (wild): not only Bigfoot's Thanksgiving dinner but also readily available anytime.

Video: turn on camera and press record.

View: nothing better than being on a mountain top!

Wind: wrecks camp in the blink of an eye.

Wood knock: I don't know what it means!

About The Author

Kevin Llewellyn grew up in Eastern Washington State and currently lives in Spokane, Washington with his wife, Carol. He graduated from Washington State University College of Veterinary Medicine. Now retired, he was a veterinarian for thirty five years, owning his own practice for twenty eight years.

He has camped, fished and hunted all his life.

At ten years old, he saw Roger Patterson in person present the Patterson-Gimlin film at the

Spokane Coliseum in Spokane, Washington. He was immediately hooked and has been following the topic of Bigfoot since. Kevin got Roger Patterson's autograph that night not knowing it would be a tiny but significant piece of history in the timeline of the Bigfoot topic. Kevin also became a member of Roger's Northwest Research Association and received bulletins/newsletters. Kevin put those aside with many other articles about Bigfoot and years later they are also a rare part of Bigfoot history. Kevin donated these items to the North American Bigfoot Center in Boring, Oregon.

Through all the years, every time Kevin is in the woods, he has kept open the possibility of Bigfoot activity occurring. He has had many and varied encounters over his decades of following the Bigfoot topic.

Kevin previously authored **Incessantly Bigfooting**.